Susan V. Bosak

With original illustrations by fifteen
internationally acclaimed artists

A TALE OF WONDER, WISDOM

DRE

tcp.

TCP Press
Toronto

dream \ drēm \ *(verb &) noun:*
    1 (to experience) a series of thoughts, images,
      or emotions when you're sleeping.
        2 (to think of) something wonderful or beautiful.
          3 (to indulge in) a fantasy created by your
            imagination while you're awake.
              4 a (to consider as a possibility) a cherished
                desire or wish for the future, or
                  b (to indulge in) a fantastic but unrealistic hope.
                    5 (to conceive of) a strong aspiration or goal.
                      6 (to live with) a sense of meaning that fills
                        your mind, makes your feet dance,
                          and stirs your soul to soar.

WISHES

WHAT'S YOUR DREAM?

I STARTED OUT JUST LIKE YOU

Once, long ago when all the stars
were born, I was a baby.

My favorite color was yellow,
the color of the sun that peeked
in my window in the morning.

When you're a baby,
you're cuddled and comforted
in your own cozy little world.
You smile and gurgle
and fuss and cry
and get fed and need changing
and sleep and dream.

DREAM A DREAM WITH ME

"We shall not cease from exploration
And the end of all our exploring
Will be to arrive where we started
And know the place for the first time."
~T.S. ELIOT

When my legs began to take me places,
my favorite colors were BRIGHT—
like rip-roaring red!

There's a whole world to explore:
Watching bubbles burst in your bath.
Tasting honey on toast.
Smelling every single flower in the garden.
Listening to laughter and thunder.
Touching your mother's face—
and your very own toes.

DREAM A DREAM WITH ME

*"Whoever would one day learn to fly must
first learn to stand and walk and run and
climb and dance; one cannot fly into flying."*
~FRIEDRICH NIETZSCHE

As I got bigger,
   my favorite colors were those of a rainbow –
   like the violet arc across the sky so real
   I could almost reach up and touch it.

There's a whole world to imagine...
Castles in your backyard.
Pumpkins transformed into gilded carriages.
Fairy friends who play with you all day.
Monsters that crouch in dark corners at night!
Wishes you make on stars.

DREAM A DREAM WITH ME

"The Possible's slow fuse is lit
By the Imagination."
~EMILY DICKINSON

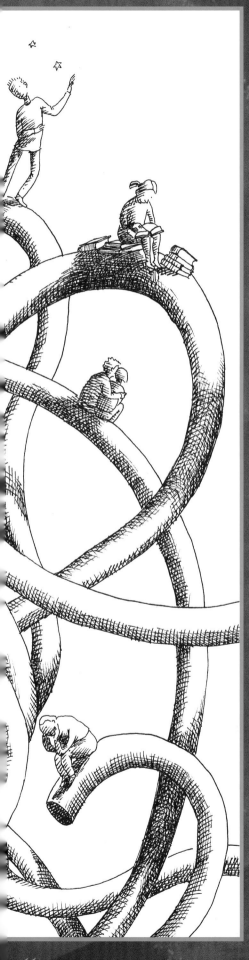

When I became a teenager,
   I liked blue.
      Everyone likes blue.

   There's a whole world to figure out.
      You think about *finally* growing up –
      Who you are
      What's important
      Where you're going
      Why you're going there
      When the right time is
      How it all fits together.

      And you think about
         having a good time along the way.

DREAM A DREAM WITH ME

"The difficulty in life
is the choice."
~ GEORGE MOORE

Then I was a grownup,
   young and strong.
   My favorite colors
   were simple black and white.
   It was easy to tell Yes from No.

   There's a whole world to conquer
      and you know exactly what you want:
      To make your own way.
      To be okay.
      To belong.
      To know things.
      To be you – and make a mark on the world.

DREAM A DREAM WITH ME

AND ALL
THAT CAME
   BEFORE...

*"It is not the mountain we conquer,
but ourselves."*

~SIR EDMUND HILLARY
FIRST PERSON TO CLIMB MT. EVEREST

Great men and great women –
some famous, most not…

"You cannot hope to build a better world without improving the individuals. To that end, each of us must work for our own improvement and, at the same time, share a general responsibility for all humanity."
~MARIE CURIE

Great ideas –
    the impossible made possible...

16

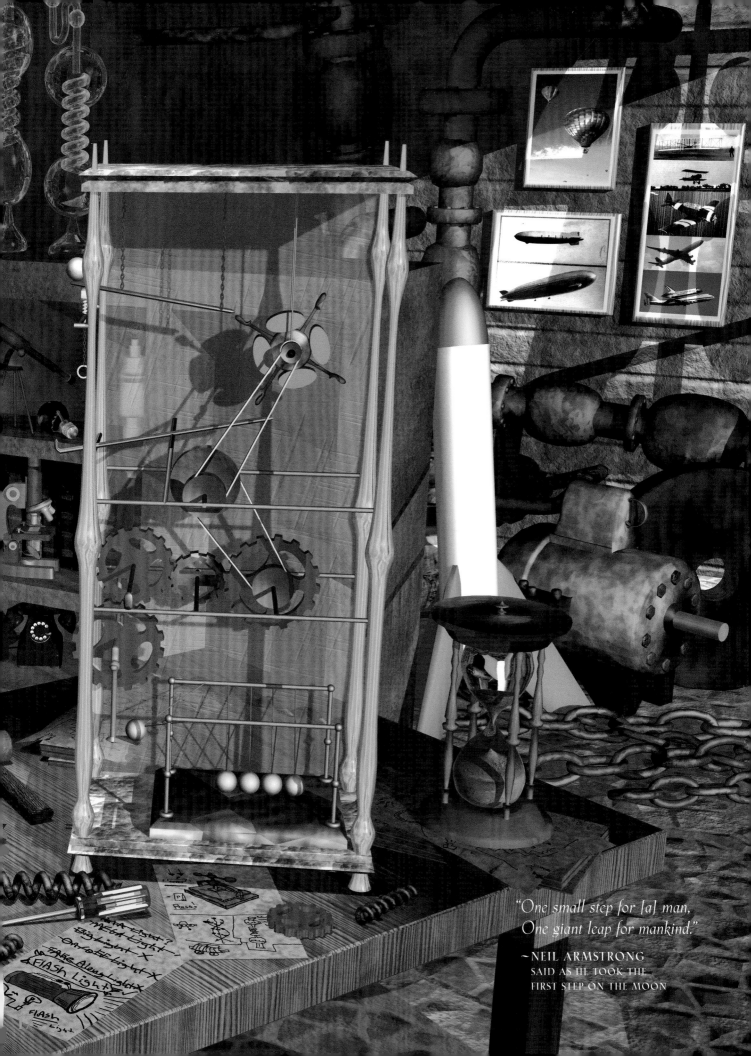

"One small step for [a] man,
One giant leap for mankind."

~NEIL ARMSTRONG
SAID AS HE TOOK THE
FIRST STEP ON THE MOON

Great hopes and joys,
fears and sorrows,
and all the living in between.

"I have a dream that my four little children will one day live in a nation where they will not be judged by the color of their skin but by the content of their character. I have a dream today!"
~MARTIN LUTHER KING JR.

But as the days became years that spun by,
my simple black-and-white world
turned gray —
the color of a dismal day.

You hear so many voices,
"No way," they say, "You're dreaming!"
Or to yourself you say,
"Things weren't supposed to be this way."
You get tired, or maybe confused or scared.
Maybe there's just too much —
too big, too long, too hard.

All you want to do is hide your head
under the covers of your bed.

"In dreams begins responsibility."
~WILLIAM BUTLER YEATS

It was gray, gray, gray.
I didn't like the gray.
Then something happened.
It will always happen – if you're looking.

It might be a smile, a wink, a nod
from someone you don't know.
It might be a hug
from someone who loves you.
It might be a word or an idea
carried on the wind from others.
Or it might be a little nudge
from deep inside you,
 "Get up!"

And then you understand –
 the secret to dreaming a dream, that is.

*"It is better to light a candle
than to curse the darkness."*

~ELEANOR ROOSEVELT
HER PHILOSOPHY AS DESCRIBED
BY ADLAI STEVENSON

I was older and strong once again.
My favorite color was green—
the color of Go and the color of Grow.

I understood that the world at its best
is green.
Dreams grow like seeds.
They need to take root,
then stretch toward the sun.
They grow slowly.
They must be tended to.
And sometimes a gray day
gives them just the rain they need.

There's something else too…

*"A hundred million miracles
Are happening every day."*

~OSCAR HAMMERSTEIN II
LYRICS FROM THE
FLOWER DRUM SONG

I understood that to grow a dream
you need more than the one I was.
You need
the Believe of childhood,
the Do of youth,
and the Think of experience.
You need all three.

There's the wisdom to fill a tooth,
simple and not so simple all at once:
Believe, Do, Think.

So,

DREAM A DREAM WITH ME

*"Chance favors only the mind
that is prepared."*
~LOUIS PASTEUR

Now I am very, very old.
My favorite color? Yellow —
the color of the billion billion stars
that sparkle in the night sky.

I have dreamed a lifetime of dreams.
I reached many of them —
not all, but many.
Many also changed along the way.
What I have most are fine memories.

When you're as old as I am
you still dream dreams.
But they're different.
Mostly they're wishes for those who follow.

DREAM A DREAM WITH ME

AND ALL
THAT COMES
AFTER...

"Hold fast to dreams
For if dreams die
Life is a broken-winged bird
That cannot fly."

~LANGSTON HUGHES

Look up, up, up
into those billion billion sparkling stars.
What dreams do you find?

Little dreams, big dreams,
each a hope looking for a life to make it real—
a life like yours.

Be a dreamer.

With everything around you,
With everything before and after you,
With everything that *is* you...

DREAM A DREAM.

YOUR VERY OWN DREAM.

EXPLORE THE ILLUSTRATIONS

Wayne Anderson

Leicestershire, England. Watercolor, ink, and colored pencil. Thousands and thousands of years ago, an ancient people carefully crafted the Dream Chest. One night, they set it on the top of a mountain. They called to the universe. A shooting star flashed across the dark sky. It swirled down to earth, circled around the chest, then burst into the chest through the carved star on its scooped lid. The Dream Chest became a magical portal between reality and dreams, what is and what can be. Mr. Anderson enjoys adding a touch of magic to his illustrations. Winner of the National Art Library Illustration Award, he also received a Gold Medal from the Society of Illustrators for *Ratsmagic*, a book he wrote and illustrated. His other books include *The Tin Forest* and *The Dragon Machine*, both by Helen Ward. "After college, I tried to get work as a graphic designer. At one interview someone suggested that because of the strong illustration bias in my portfolio that maybe I should pursue a career as an illustrator. I was unaware that it would be possible to make a living creating pictures. Dreams can come true!"

Steve Johnson and Lou Fancher

Minneapolis, MN. Oil on paper. While wandering a barren desert, a traveler comes upon the Dream Chest at the end of a rainbow. The chest has a curious carved star on its scooped lid. The traveler opens the chest. A wise old star emerges (a symbol of the eternal spirit and a mentor figure) and whisks the traveler away on the journey of a lifetime. The story ends with the

---

Dream Star encouraging both the traveler and the reader to pursue their own dreams. The birds in the two final illustrations tie to the Langston Hughes quotation on page 29. This husband-and-wife team takes a collaborative approach in which both artists conceive, draw, design, and paint. Their 25 books together include *I Walk at Night* (Lois Duncan), a New York Times Best Illustrated Book, along with Dr. Seuss's *My Many Colored Days* and *The Boy on Fairfield Street: How Ted Geisel Grew Up to Become Dr. Seuss* (Kathleen Krull). "We always look for art. We see it in the night sky, the glow of light on a child's face, the magic of a good story, the fantastic world of dreams."

Christian Birmingham

London, England. Chalk pastels on brown pastel paper. A baby reaches up to the stars in a mobile. The eye-level point of view suggests the watchful eyes of a parent. Two of Mr. Birmingham's most widely known books are *The Night Before Christmas* (Clement C. Moore) and *The Classic Tales of Hans Christian Andersen* (Margaret Clark). Shortlisted for several awards, including the Kate Greenaway and Kurt Maschler Awards, he won the Whitbread Children's Book of the Year. "It was seeing the work of Edmund Dulac in *Tales from the Arabian Nights* that inspired me to pursue illustration as a career. I can't imagine any child who has seen Dulac's illustrations wanting to do anything other than illustrate."

Barbara Reid

Toronto, Canada. 3-D plasticine, photographed. A playful perspective on a toddler ties to the five senses suggested by the text. The puzzle toy, with the red star cutout and the yellow star shape, is based on one Ms. Reid's daughters played with as young children. In addition to illustrating many books, she wrote and illustrated *Subway Mouse* and *The Party*, which won the Governor General's Award. Her other

---

honors include the Ezra Jack Keats Award. "When I was about eight, my grandfather gave me a fairly advanced drawing kit. He told me it was because I was an artist. I had never thought of myself that way. His confidence gave me confidence."

Zhong-Yang Huang

Regina, Canada. Watercolor with colored pencil. A celebration of stories and the imagination, the characters in the illustration are: Aladdin and his magic lamp, riding on a flying carpet; Tinker Bell from *Peter Pan*, with stars swirling off her magic wand; Cinderella, from one of the best-known fairy tales in the world; the Monkey King, a superhero character from Chinese legend who can transform into 72 different images and travel one hundred thousand miles in one somersault; Anansi the Spider, a trickster-hero character from African folklore; the Tin Woodman, Lion, and Scarecrow from *The Wizard of Oz*; the tortoise and the hare from Aesop's fables; and Jack and the ogre from *Jack and the Beanstalk*. Nominated twice for the Governor General's Award, Mr. Huang won the Amelia Frances Howard-Gibbon Illustrator's Award for *The Dragon New Year* (David Bouchard). His art was also honored with the Silver Medal at the Sixth National Fine Art Exhibition of China. His other books include *The Great Race* and *The Mermaid's Muse*, also by David Bouchard. "I drew from the time I was four years old. When I was fifteen, I was forced to leave school and sent to be a field laborer during the Chinese Cultural Revolution. Only painting could make me feel happy during this time. I had some art books and taught myself. Once the revolution was over, I was able to continue my formal studies in fine art."

Michèle Lemieux

Montreal, Canada. Ink on paper. The tangled mass represents

---

outer choices and also the "inner architecture" that evolves as we live and learn. A boy juggles stars in the upper-right corner. Ms. Lemieux has illustrated many books in a variety of mediums. She both illustrated and wrote *Stormy Night*, which has been translated into fourteen languages, won the prestigious Bologna Ragazzi Award, and was made into an animated film that won the Crystal Bear Award at the Berlin Film Festival. "If I was stranded alone on an island, I would build something with my hands, even if no one ever saw it. I have a need to create, to be a part of life and leave something behind."

Shaun Tan

Perth, Australia. Acrylic, oil, and collage. A young woman forges a path up a mountain on what seems like a straightforward route, while hidden ahead are more complex choices (symbolized by the signpost before the summit). Her smiling face (eyes, nose, and mouth) is echoed in the landscape, showing that we are a part of the world and the world is a part of us. She carries a scroll in her hand, perhaps a map or diploma, and a small flowering plant in her knapsack, ready to be planted in an appropriate place. The hopeful image of the birds foreshadows the Langston Hughes quotation on page 29. The mountain's collage texture is made up of bits of maps, symbols, and text in different languages, suggesting culture, history, learning, and experience. A star is hidden in the mountain, toward the top. In the distance on one side is the flaming beacon of the Lighthouse of Alexandria, one of the ancient wonders of the world. On the other side is Big Ben, which many consider a modern wonder. These symbols of light and time remind us that even the smallest personal journey (the story text references psychologist Abraham Maslow's hierarchy of human needs) lies within the greater narrative of human passage from past to present. Mr. Tan received the CBCA Picture Book of the Year Award for *The Rabbits* (John Marsden). He both wrote and illustrated *The Red Tree*, winner of a "Prix Octogones," as well as *The*

Lost Thing, which received a Bologna Book Fair Honorable Mention. He was also named Best Artist at the World Fantasy Awards. "Things seem impossible only because of a failure of imagination and patience, which are more important tools when facing a problem than simply having knowledge. What makes art and literature so interesting is that they present us with unusual things that encourage us to ask questions about what we think we know."

James Bennett

Bucks County, PA. Oil on board. Those who have come before us have laid the foundation for the ideas and dreams of today. Front, left to right: Rachel Carson, Leonardo da Vinci, Albert Einstein, Anne Frank (wearing the yellow star), Mohandas Gandhi, William Shakespeare, Ludwig van Beethoven, Charlie Chaplin, Margaret Mead, Harold Allen (a youth mentor with Experience Corps in Philadelphia, PA, representing the ordinary person who can make a difference), Sojourner Truth. Rear, left to right: Ferdinand Magellan, Simón Bolívar, Amelia Earhart, Nicholas Copernicus, Confucius, Socrates. Mr. Bennett's awards include Gold Medals from the Society of Illustrators and the Hamilton King Award. His other books include *Halloween* (Jerry Seinfeld) and *Tell Me a Scary Story...But Not Too Scary!* (Carl Reiner). "I approach life and art in the same way: sometimes you need to exaggerate something, make it bigger than life, to really see it."

Bruce Wood

Kailua Kona, HI. 3-D digital. Some of the key inventions and discoveries in this alchemist-inspired lab, from left to right: fire (candles on wall); printing press; computer (keyboard); the table under the window includes batteries, a perpetual motion machine (yet to be perfected!), and a television (showing lunar landing); the central table includes CDs, futuristic flat-screen viewer (showing Apollo 11 liftoff), calculator, notebook (with

a sketch of a rocket surrounded by stars), simple DNA model, gears, flashlight (sheet of paper lists options for naming this invention), a Rube Goldberg–inspired device with a Newton's Cradle, and an hourglass; toward the rear wall is a test rocket, electric motor, and wheel; pictures on the wall show the history of flight from the hot air balloon and dirigible to the prop plane, jet plane, and space shuttle; shelves in the middle rear of the illustration store a spyglass, light bulbs, microscope, and telephone. Mr. Wood is a fifth-generation artist, the son of children's author Audrey Wood and illustrator Don Wood, and the grandson of artist Edwin Brewer. His children's books, written by Audrey Wood, have earned critical acclaim. They include *Ten Little Fish*, *Alphabet Adventure*, and *Alphabet Mystery*. "I'm using a medium that allows me to combine all the things I enjoy the most. When designing on a computer, I use elements of drama, art, photography, drawing, painting, and sculpture. The computer can be a very creative tool."

Robert Ingpen

Born Geelong, Australia. Drybrush watercolor. A central guiding star illuminates the entire illustration. As St. George slays the dragon on one side and a mother cradles her child on the other, the central image of a mime represents the peak of human performance and statement. A soldier tucked in the crook of the mime's arm represents the reality of ever-present dangers, while the hopeful, life-giving gesture of the mime's hand carries (from left to right) the heroic defense of right over might; the celebration of achievement; learning and literature (woman reading a letter, after Vermeer); and the basic worship of nature and religion. Mr. Ingpen's prolific career encompasses more than 100 books, including the classic *Lifetimes* (Bryan Mellonie) and the recent *Halloween Circus* (Charise Neugebauer). In his long list of awards is the prestigious Hans Christian Andersen Medal for Children's Literature. "I follow, as best I can, the paths cut out at previous times by storytellers, inventors, writers, and artists. These tracks mark the search by

someone who may be looking for an explanation, a plot, a challenge that cannot be found other than in the mind."

Raúl Colón

New City, NY. Colored pencil, watercolor wash, and scratching. Achieving dreams often requires the courage to overcome obstacles and fears. A navigational star appears in the clock/compass on the bedside table. It is implied behind the spinning hands in the first illustration. Mr. Colón's awards include Silver and Gold Medals from the Society of Illustrators. *My Mama Had a Dancing Heart* (Libba Moore Gray) was selected as a New York Times Best Illustrated Book. His other books include *Orson Blasts Off!*, which he both wrote and illustrated, and *Tomás and the Library Lady* (Pat Mora). "As a child I had chronic asthma and would frequently be so ill that I could not leave the house for days or even weeks at a time. But all those times I spent locked up inside, I spent filling up dozens of composition notebooks with all kinds of drawings. So my illness as a child, which kept me from going outside to play, became a blessing."

Leo and Diane Dillon

New York, NY. Acrylic on acetate with oil glaze. The person and the dream become one reaching toward the sun (which is a star). In the second illustration, all generations – symbolizing the Believe, Do, Think of realizing dreams – work together to harvest fruit as the Dream Tree embraces them as a unified community. The older woman wears a star pendant. She crafts floral wreaths, one of which the young girl wears on her head, representing the gifts passed across generations and how older mentors can help the young achieve their goals. Believe, Do, Think has multiple meanings: 1) pursuing a dream requires believing in it, acting upon it, and making strategic, thoughtful choices; 2) there must be a unity of spirit, body, and mind; 3) we need

psychological/social qualities from all stages of life – childhood, young adulthood, and older adulthood – to succeed; and 4) we need to learn from the past, live fully in the present, and hope for the future. The Dillons, a husband–and–wife team, have devoted their lives to art and to the craft of illustration. They view their unique collaboration as the "third artist," able to achieve things neither individual could alone. In 1997, they celebrated their fortieth anniversary and completed their fortieth book, *To Every Thing There Is a Season*. Awarded the Caldecott Medal twice (for *Ashanti to Zulu* by Margaret Musgrove and *Why Mosquitoes Buzz in People's Ears* by Verna Aardema), their long list of honors also includes two Coretta Scott King Awards and being inducted into the Society of Illustrators Hall of Fame. "We all have a lot in common. It is our beliefs that divide us. We have little control over what life brings us, but we can change our thoughts."

Mike Carter

Toronto, Canada. Digital. The "From Reality to Dreams" series of images created for the colored page backgrounds starts with a sprinkling of stars, moves through the tumult of a sandstorm, and ends with a page overflowing with stars. Mr. Carter also created the endpapers. Recipient of the Duke of Edinburgh Award (Gold), he has done artwork for hundreds of advertising, editorial, and design projects. "I'm living my dream – I draw for a living. It's taken thousands of hours of drawing and repetition to learn my craft. I'm happy I attained my childhood goal. Much more of the same, please!"

The questions on these pages are adapted from Visual Thinking Strategies developed by Philip Yenawine and Abigail Housen. The first question encourages children to share their individual observations, while the second prompts closer examination to support interpretations. "What more can we find?" broadens the discussion for a group, or for an adult and child, to make even more discoveries together. For more information and activities, visit www.legacyproject.org.

DREAM

For my mother, Nadia Bosak, who loves to look up at the stars.

Published by

TCP Press
9 Lobraico Lane
Whitchurch-Stouffville, ON
L4A 7X5 Canada
(905) 640-8914
www.tcppress.com

Publishing Coordination
Brian A. Puppa

Production
Douglas A. Bosak

Book Design
Pylon, www.pylondesign.ca

Printing and Binding
Friesens, www.friesens.com

The text type is set in Phaistos.
The book is printed on
acid-free paper.

National Library of Canada
Cataloguing in Publication

Bosak, Susan V.
Dream : a tale of wonder,
wisdom & wishes / written by
Susan V. Bosak ; illustrated by
15 internationally acclaimed
artists.

ISBN 1-896232-04-3

I. Title.

PS8553.O7365D74 2004
jC813'.54   C2004-902318-7

Printed in Canada
08 07 06 05 04
10 9 8 7 6 5 4 3 2 1

Are You a DREAMer?

The Legacy Project's LifeDreams initiative helps you find and fulfill your dreams. Get free online activity kits, guides, tip sheets, and books. Participate in essay contests, workshops, and more.

The *Dream* book is the starting point for LifeDreams. You're never too young or too old to dream! No matter what stage of life you're in, LifeDreams takes you to the next step with inspiration, insights, and information on living your dreams and making a difference. For parents and grandparents, there are also fun activities and ideas for opening thoughtful discussions with children and teens about dreams and goals. For teachers and youth leaders, there are learning springboards into areas from career and financial planning to language arts and life skills.

The Legacy Project is about creating your life – learning from the past, living fully in the present, and building toward the future. It's an international community service program of TCP with the nonprofit Parenting Coalition and Generations United, both based in Washington, DC. Proceeds from *Dream* help support the Legacy Project.

VISIT OUR INTERACTIVE WEBSITE

Free online intergenerational LifeDreams activity kits include activities, self-assessments, games, creative crafts, art projects (with more about the illustrations in *Dream*), lesson ideas, plus practical information, reproducibles, and listings of recommended books and resources. Join the Club of Dreamers – some of the members are illustrated on pages 14-15! You can also add a story about your hopes and goals to the World Dream Chest, and read the moving, motivating stories from others.

MAKE A WISH ON THE DREAM STAR IN PERSON

Traveling coast to coast, the LifeDreams Exhibit is an entertaining, educational multimedia experience for children and adults. Be inspired by famous dreamers and achievers throughout history. Find out your personal Dreamer Profile. Peek into the beautifully handcrafted Dream Chest to catch a glimpse of the "stars" inside. See what happens when you wish on the magical Dream Star! And delight in viewing all the original, full-scale works of art created for *Dream*.

COUNT THE STARS AND WIN!

There's at least one star hidden in each illustration in *Dream*. When you find a star, don't forget to make a new wish each time! Count all the stars and enter your total on the Legacy Project website to win some five-star prizes. Complete details are at www.legacyproject.org.